# Are You Sad, Mama?

# Are You Sad, Mama?

## by Elizabeth Winthrop

### illustrated by Donna Diamond

Harper & Row, Publishers

New York, Hagerstown, San Francisco, London

ARE YOU SAD, MAMA?
Text copyright © 1979 by Elizabeth Winthrop Mahony
Illustrations copyright © 1979 by Donna Diamond
All rights reserved. No part of this book may be used or reproduced in any manner
whatsoever without written permission except in the case of brief quotations em-
bodied in critical articles and reviews. Printed in the United States of America. For
information address Harper & Row, Publishers, Inc., 10 East 53rd Street, New York,
N.Y. 10022. Published simultaneously in Canada by Fitzhenry & Whiteside Limited,
Toronto.
FIRST EDITION

Library of Congress Cataloging in Publication Data
Winthrop, Elizabeth.
  Are you sad, Mama?

  SUMMARY: A little girl tries to cheer up her
sad mother.
  [1. Sadness—Fiction.  2. Emotions—Fiction.
3. Mothers and daughters—Fiction]  I. Diamond,
Donna.  II. Title.
PZ7.W768Ar 1979        [E]        77-25661
ISBN 0-06-026539-6
ISBN 0-06-026544-2 lib. bdg.

**For Eliza**
**who makes me happy**

Once there was a little girl whose mother was very sad.
"Are you sad, Mama?" asked the little girl.
"Yes," said her mama.

"I will read you a book, Mama,"
said the little girl.
"Maybe that will make you happy.
Once upon a time,
there was a fuzzy brown bear.
See, Mama, look at the picture.
He looks just like my bear."
But her mother did not want
to look at the picture.
She was still very sad.
So the little girl put away the book.

"I will jump for you, Mama,"
said the little girl.
"Maybe that will make you happy."
So the little girl jumped up and down.
"That does not make me happy,"
said her mother.
"That makes me dizzy."
So the little girl stopped jumping.

"I will sing you a song, Mama.
That will make you happy."
So the little girl sang a song about the moon.
"That's a nice song," said her mother.
"But it makes me feel sad."
So the little girl stopped singing.

"I will draw you a picture, Mama.
That will make you happy."
So the little girl drew a picture
of the sun and four rabbits.
"That's a pretty picture," said her mother.
But her face was still sad.
So the little girl put away her crayons.

"I will get you something to eat, Mama.
That will make you happy."
So the little girl brought her mother two cookies.
"Thank you," said her mother.
"But I am not hungry."
So the little girl ate the cookies herself.

"I will bring you my bear, Mama.
Maybe that will make you happy."
So the little girl sat her fuzzy brown bear
in her mother's lap.
"Hello, Bear," said her mother.
She touched his chewed off ear
and his button nose.
But her face looked sadder than ever.
So the little girl put away her bear.

"I will brush your hair, Mama.
Maybe that will make you happy."
So the little girl brushed her mother's hair.
"Ouch, that pulls," said her mother,
and her eyes filled with tears.
So the little girl put away the hairbrush.

"I will go away and leave you alone, Mama.
Maybe that will make you happy."
"Oh, no," cried her mother.
"If you go away, that will make me cry."
So the little girl put her arms
around her mother's neck and
hugged her tight.

"Oh, yes," said her mother.
"This does make me happy."
"This makes me happy, too, Mama,"
said the little girl.